A Tramp Through the Bret Harte Country

Thomas Dykes Beasley

Contents

A TRAMP THROUGH THE BRET HARTE COUNTRY

BY

Thomas Dykes Beasley

Foreword

In California's imaginary Hall of Fame, Bret Harte must be accorded a prominent, if not first place. His short stories and dialect poems published fifty years ago made California well known the world over and gave it a romantic interest conceded no other community. He saw the picturesque and he made the world see it. His power is unaccountable if we deny him genius. He was essentially an artist. His imagination gave him vision, a new life in beautiful setting supplied colors and rare literary skill painted the picture.

His capacity for absorption was marvelous. At the age of about twenty he spent less than a year in the foot-hills of the Sierras, among pioneer miners, and forty-five years of literary output did not exhaust his impressions. He somewhere refers to an "eager absorption of the strange life around me, and a photographic sensitiveness, to certain scenes and incidents." "Eager absorption," "photographic sensitiveness," a rich imagination and a fine literary style, largely due to his mother, enabled him to win at his death this acknowledgment from the "London Spectator:" "No writer of the present day has struck so powerful and original a note as he has sounded."

Francis Bret Harte was born in Albany, New York, August 25, 1836. His father was a teacher and translator; his mother a woman of high character and cultivated tastes. His father having died, he, when nine, became an office boy and later a clerk. In 1854 he came to California to join his mother who had married again, arriving in Oakland in March of that year. His employment for two years was desultory. He worked in a drug store and also wrote for Eastern magazines. Then he went to Alamo in the San Ramon Valley as tutor--a valued experience. Later in 1856 he went to Tuolumne County where, among other things, he taught school, and may have been an express messenger. At any rate, he stored his memory with material that ten years later made him and the whole region famous.

In 1857 he went to Humboldt County where his sister was living. He was an interesting figure, gentlemanly, fastidious, reserved, sensitive, with a good fund of humor, a pleasant voice and a modest manner. He seemed poorly fitted for anything that needed doing. He was willing, for I saw him digging post holes and building a fence with results somewhat unsatisfactory. He was more successful as tutor for two of my boy friends. He finally became printers' devil in the office of the "Northern Californian," where he learned the case, and incidentally contributed graceful verse and clever prose.

He returned to San Francisco early in 1860 and found work on the "Golden Era," at first as compositor and soon as writer. In May, 1864, he left the "Golden Era" and joined others in starting "The Californian." Two months later he was made editor of the new "Overland Monthly." The second number contained "The Luck of Roaring Camp." It attracted wide attention as a new note. Other stories and poems of merit followed. Harte's growing reputation burst in full bloom when in 1870 he filled a blank space in the "Overland" make-up with "The Heathen Chinee." It was quoted on the floor of the Senate and gained world-wide fame. He received flattering offers and felt constrained to accept the best. In February, 1871, he left California. A Boston publisher had offered him $10,000 for whatever he might write in the following year. Harte accepted, but the output was small.

For seven years he wrote spasmodically, eking out his income by lecturing and newspaper work. Life was hard. In 1878 he sailed for Europe, having been appointed consular agent at Crefeld, Prussia, about forty miles north of Cologne. In 1880 he was made Consul at Glasgow, where he remained five years. His home thereafter was London, where he continued his literary work until his death in March, 1902.

His complete works comprise nineteen volumes. His patriotic verse is fervid, his idyls are graceful and his humorous verse delightful. The short story he made anew.

Harte's instincts and habits were good. He had the artistic temperament and some of its incidental weaknesses. He acknowledged himself "constitutionally improvident," and a debt-burdened life is not easy. His later years were pathetic. Those who knew and appreciated him remember him fondly. California failing to know him, wrongs herself.

Charles A. Murdock.

Preface

A desire to obtain, at first hand, any possible information in regard to reminiscences of Bret Harte, Mark Twain and others of the little coterie of writers, who in the early fifties visited the mining camps of California and through stories that have become classics, played a prominent part in making "California" a synonym for romance, led to undertaking the tramp of which this brief narrative is a record. The writer met with unexpected success, having the good fortune to meet men, all over eighty years of age, who had known--in some cases intimately Bret Harte, Mark Twain, "Dan de Quille," Prentice Mulford, Bayard Taylor and Horace Greeley.

It seems imperative that a relation of individual experiences--however devoid of stirring incident and adventure--should be written in the first person. At the same time, the writer of this unpretentious story of a summer's tramp cannot but feel that he owes his readers--should he have any an apology for any avoidable egotism. His excuse is that, no twit notwithstanding ding the glamour attaching to the old mining towns, it is almost incredible how little is known of them by the average Californian; for the Eastern tourist there is more excuse, since the foot-hills of the Sierras lie outside the beaten tracks of travel. He has, therefore, assumed that "a plain unvarnished tale" of actual experiences might not be without interest to the casual reader; and possibly might incite in him a desire to see for himself a country not only possessed of rare beauty, but absolutely unique in its associations.

But the point to be emphasized is that the glamour is not a thing of the past: it is there now. Nay, to a person possessed of any imagination, the ruins--say, of Coloma--appeal in all probability far stronger than would the actual town itself in the days when it seethed with bustle and excitement. Not to have visited the old mining towns is not to have seen the "heart" of California, or felt its pulsations. It is not to understand why the very name "California" still stirs the blood and excites the imagination throughout the civilized world.

If this brief narrative should induce anyone to "gird up his loins," shoulder his pack and essay a similar pilgrimage, the author will feel that he has not been unrewarded. And if a man over threescore years of age can tramp through seven counties and return, in spite of intense heat, feeling better and stronger than when he started, a young fellow in the hey-day of life and sound of wind and limb surely ought not to be discouraged.

Thomas Dykes Beasley.

A Tramp Through the Bret Harte Country
Chapter I

Reminiscences of Bret Harte. "Plain Language From Truthful James." The Glamour of the Old Mining Towns

It is forty-four years since the writer met the author of "The Luck of Roaring Camp"--that wonderful blending within the limits of a short story of humor, pathos and tragedy--which, incredible as it may seem, met with but a cold reception from the local press, and was even branded as "indecent" and "immodest!"

On the occasion referred to, I was strolling on Rincon Hill--at that time the fashionable residence quarter of San Francisco--in company with Mr. J. H. Wildes, whose cousin, the late Admiral Frank Wildes, achieved fame in the battle of Manila Bay. Mr. Wildes called my attention to an approaching figure and said: "Here comes Bret Harte, a man of unusual literary ability. He is having a hard struggle now, but only needs the opportunity, to make a name for himself."

That opportunity arrived almost immediately. In the September number of the Overland Monthly, 1870, of which magazine Mr. Harte was then editor, appeared "Plain Language from Truthful James," or "The Heathen Chinee," as the poem was afterwards called. A few weeks later, to my amazement, while turning the pages of Punch in the Mercantile Library, I came across "The Heathen Chinee;" an unique compliment so far as my recollection of Punch serves. To this generous and instantaneous recognition of genius may be attributed in no small measure the rapid distinction won by Bret Harte in the world of letters.

Mr. Harte read his "Heathen Chinee" to Mrs. Wildes, some time before it was published. This lady, a woman of brilliant attainments and one who had a host of friends in old San Francisco, possessed the keenest sense of humor. Mr. Harte greatly valued her critical judgment. He was in the habit of reading his stories and poems to her for her opinion and decision, before publication, and it may well be that her hearty laughter and warm approval helped to strengthen his wavering opinion of the lines which convulsed Anglo-Saxondom; for no one was more surprised than he at the sensation they created. He had even offered the poem for publication to Mr. Ambrose Bierce, then editing the San Francisco News Letter; but Mr. Bierce, recognizing its merit, returned it to Mr. Harte and prevailed upon him to publish it in his own magazine.

Had one at that time encountered Mr. Harte in Piccadilly or Fifth Avenue, he would simply have been aware of a man dressed in perfect taste, but in the height of the prevailing fashion. On the streets of San Francisco, however, Bret Harte was always a notable figure, from the fact that the average man wore "slops," devoid alike of style or cut, and usually of shiny broadcloth. Broad-brimmed black felt hats were the customary headgear, completing a most funereal costume.

Mr. Harte impressed me as being singularly modest and utterly devoid of any form of affectation. To be well dressed in a period when little attention was paid clothes by the San Franciscan, might, it is true, in some men have suggested assumption of an air of superiority; but with Mr. Harte, to dress well was simply a natural instinct. His long, drooping moustache and the side-whiskers of the time--incongruous as the comparison may seem--called to mind the elder Sothern as "Lord Dundreary." His natural expression was pensive, even sad. When one considers that pathos and tragedy, perhaps even more than humor, pervade his stories, that was not surprising.

I had but recently arrived from England--a mere lad. California was still the land of gold and romance; the glamour with which Bret Harte surrounded both, that bids fair to be immortal, held me enthralled. Angel's, Rough and Ready, Sandy Bar, Poker Flat, Placerville, Tuolumne and old Sonora represented to me enchanted ground. Fate and life's vicissitudes prevented, except in imagination, a knowledge of the Sierra foot-hill counties; but in the back of my head all these years had persisted a determination to, at some time, visit a region close to the heart of every old Californian, and what better way than on foot?

In spite of Pullman cars and automobiles--or, rather, perhaps on account of them--the only way to see a country, to get into touch with Nature and meet the inhabitants on the dead level of equality and human sympathy, is to use Nature's method of locomotion. Equipped with a stout stick--with a view to dogs--a folding kodak camera, and your "goods and chattels" slung in a haversack across your shoulders, you feel independent of timecards and "routes;" and sally forth into the world with the philosophical determination to take things as they come; keyed to a pleasurable pitch of excitement by the knowledge that "Adventure" walks with you hand-in-hand, and that the "humors of the road" are yours for the seeing and understanding.

Chapter II
Inception of the Tramp. Stockton to Angel's Camp. Tuttletown and the "Sage of Jackass Hill"

Following as near as might be the route of the old Argonauts, I avoided trains, and on a warm summer night boarded the Stockton boat. In the early morning you are aware of slowly rounding the curves of the San Joaquin River. Careful steering was most essential, as owing to the dry season the river was unusually low. The vivid greens afforded by the tules and willows that fringe the river banks, and the occasional homestead surrounded by trees, with its little landing on the edge of the levee, should delight the eye of the artist.

I lost no time in Stockton and headed for Milton in the foot-hills, just across the western boundary of Calaveras County. The distance was variously estimated by the natives at from twenty to forty miles--Californians are careless about distances, as in other matters. Subsequently I entered it in my note book as a long twenty-eight. Eighteen miles out from Stockton, at a place called Peters, which is little more than a railway junction, you leave the cultivated land and enter practically a desert country, destitute of water, trees, undergrowth and with but a scanty growth of grass. I ate my lunch at the little store and noted with apprehension that the thermometer registered 104 degrees in the shaded porch. I am not likely to forget that pull of ten miles and inwardly confessed to a regret that I had not taken the train to Milton. Accustomed on "hikes" to a thirst not surpassed by anything "east of Suez," I never before appreciated the significance of the word "parched"--the "tongue cleaving to the roof of the mouth."

At Milton one enters the land of romance. What was even more appreciable at the time, it marks the limit of the inhospitable country I had traversed. Mr. Robert Donner, the proprietor of the Milton Hotel, told me he once had "Black Bart" as his guest for over a week, being unaware at the time of his identity. This famous bandit in the early eighties "held up" the Yosemite stage time and again. In fact, he terrorized the whole Sierra country from Redding to Sacramento. He was finally captured in San Francisco through a clew obtained from a laundry mark on a pair of white cuffs. For years, Mr. Donner cherished a boot left by the highwayman in the hurry of departure, which, much to his annoyance, was finally abstracted by some person unknown. To dispose of Black Bart; he served his term and was never seen again in the Sierras. There is a rumor that Wells Fargo & Company, the chief sufferers by his activities, made it worth his while to behave himself in the future.

The following day I reached Copperopolis. This place very justly has the reputation of being one of the hottest spots in the foot-hills. Owing to resumed operations on a large scale, of the Calaveras Copper Company, I found the little settlement crowded to its fullest capacity, and was perforce compelled to resort to genuine "hobo" methods--in short, I spent the night under the lee of a haystack. My original intention had been to walk thence to Sonora, twenty-four miles; but finding the road would take me again into the valley, I decided to make for Angel's Camp, only thirteen miles away.

It is uphill nearly all the way from Copperopolis to Angel's Camp, but mostly you are in the pine woods. My spirits rose with the altitude and delight at the magnificent view when I at last reached the summit. Toiling up the grade in the dust, I met a good old-fashioned four-horse Concord stage, which from all appearances might have been in action ever since the days of Bret Harte. At last I felt I was in touch with the Sierras. The driver even honored my bow with an abrupt "Howdy!" which from such a magnate, I took to be a good omen.

In common with all the old mining towns--though I was unaware of it at the time--Angel's, as it is usually called, is situated in the ravine where gold was first discovered. It straggles down the gulch for a mile and a half. There are a number of pretty cottages clinging to the steep hillsides, surrounded with flowers and trees, the whole effect being extremely pleasing. I registered at the Angel's Hotel, built in 1852. Across the street is the Wells Fargo building, erected about the same time and of solid stone, as is the hotel. Nothing on this trip surprised me more than the solidity of the hotels and stores built in the early fifties. Instead of the flimsy wooden structures I had imagined, I found, for the most part, thick stone walls. It was evident the Pioneers believed in the permanence of the gold deposits in the Mother Lode. Possibly they were right; Angel's is anything but a dead town to-day. The Utica, Angel's and Lightner mines give employment to hundreds of men.

In the afternoon I visited the Bret Harte Girls' High School. It is a very simple frame building, on the summit of a hill overlooking the town. The man who directed me how to find it, I discovered had not the remotest idea who Bret Harte might be; "John Brown" would have answered the purpose equally as well. In fact, all through the seven counties I traversed--Tuolumne, Calaveras, Amador, El Dorado, Placer, Nevada and Yuba--I found Bret Harte had left but a hazy and nebulous impression. Mark Twain, Prentice Mulford, Horace Greeley, Bayard Taylor, even "Dan de Quille," seemed better known.

The next morning I started for Sonora. In seven miles I came to the Stanislaus River, running in a deep and splendid canon. The river here is spanned by a fine concrete bridge, built jointly by Tuolumne and Calaveras Counties, between which the river forms the dividing line. In the bottom of the canon is the Melones mine, with a mill operating one hundred stamps. The main tunnel is a mile and a half in length; the longest mining tunnel in the State, I was told.

A steep pull of two miles out of the canon brought me to Tuttletown. Here I stayed several hours, for the interest of the whole trip, so far as Bret Harte was concerned, centered around this once celebrated camp, and Jackass Hill, on which, at one time, lived James W. Gillis, the supposed prototype of "Truthful James." He died a few years ago, but his brother, Stephen R. Gillis, is living there to-day, and after some little difficulty I succeeded in finding his house.

Mr. Gillis scouts the idea that his brother "Jim" was the "Truthful James" of Bret Harte. He said that in reality it was J. W. E. Townsend, known in old times as "Alphabetical Townsend," also by the uncomplimentary appellation of "Lying Jim." According to Mr. Gillis, Bret Harte made but one visit to Tuttletown. He arrived there one evening "dead broke" and James put him up for the night and lent him money to help him on his way. Personally, Mr. Gillis never met Bret Harte but he had seen Mark Twain on a number of Occasions. I got the distinct impression that Stephen Gillis disliked the notoriety his brother had gained, through the fact that his name had become indissolubly linked with the "Truthful James" of Bret Harte's verses. Be that as it may, I later on met several men who had known "Jim" Gillis intimately and they all agreed that he possessed a keen sense of humor and had at command a practically inexhaustible stock of stories, upon which he drew at will. Whether Bret Harte derived any inspiration from "Jim" Gillis may perhaps always remain in doubt; but that Mark Twain did, there cannot, I think, be any question.

In a recent life of Bret Harte, by Henry Childs Merwin, it is stated (page 21) that in 1858 Bret Harte acted as tutor in a private family at Alamo, in the San Ramon valley, which lies at the foot of Mount Diablo. On, page 50, however, we read: "In 1858 or thereabouts, Bret Harte was teaching school at Tuttletown, a few miles north of Sonora." It would seem that this statement is erroneous, apart from the fact that it conflicts with the prior date in reference to Alamo.

Mrs. Swerer, who has lived continuously at Tuttletown since 1850, coming there at the age of ten, told me she received her education at the Tuttletown public school, as did her children and her children's children--she is now a great-grandmother! She said most positively that she never saw Bret Harte in her life, but had frequently seen "Dan de Quille" and Mark Twain. The latter, she said, made periodic visits to Tuttletown, and always stayed with "Jim" Gillis--called by Twain, the "Sage of Jackass Hill."

Mrs. Gross, who keeps the Tuttletown Hotel and whose husband owned a store across the way, built of stone but now in ruins, was born in Tuttletown. She asserted she never heard of Bret Harte being in Tuttletown and feels it to be impossible he ever taught school there. At this ancient hostelry, built of wood and dating back to the early fifties, I dined in company with an old miner, who told me he came across "Jim" Gillis in Alaska. He said: "Gillis was a great josher. For the life of me, I could never tell from his stories whether he had been to the Klondike or not."

Chapter III
Tuolumne to Placerville. Charm of Sonora and Fascination of San Andreas and Mokelumne Hill

Sonora is nine miles distant from Tuttletown, and I reached it in the early afternoon. Perhaps of all the old mining towns, Sonora is the most fascinating, on account of the exceeding beauty of the surrounding country. No matter from what direction you approach it, Sonora seems to lie basking in the sun, buried in a wealth of greenery, through which gleam white walls and roofs of houses. Even its winding streets are so shaded by graceful old trees that buildings are half hidden. The bustle and excitement of the mining days are passed forever, in all probability, for old Sonora; but in their place have come the peace and quiet that accompany the tillage of the soil; for Sonora is now the center of a prosperous agricultural district and the town maintains a steady and continuous growth.

Here I had the pleasure of an interview with Mr. John Neal, a prominent and respected citizen of Tuolumne County, who as Commissioner represented his county at the San Francisco Midwinter Fair. Mr. Neal is over eighty, but still hale and hearty. He was the first person I had thus far encountered who had known Bret Harte in the flesh. He had also known and frequently met Mark Twain, "Dan de Quille" and Prentice Mulford. Of the four, it was evident that Mulford had left by far the most lasting as well as favorable impression on his mind. Of him he spoke in terms of real affection. "Prentice Mulford," he said, "was a brilliant, very handsome and most lovable young man." I asked him how these young men were regarded by the miners. He said: "In all the camps they were held to be in a class by themselves, on account of their education and literary ability. Although they wore the rough costume of the miners, it was realized that none of them took mining seriously or made any pretense of real work with pick and shovel." Mr. Neal knew James Gillis intimately and admitted he was a great story-teller. In fact, at the bare mention of his name he broke into a hearty laugh. "Oh, Jim Gillis, he was a great fellow!" he exclaimed. He said unquestionably Mark Twain got a good deal of material from him, and feels certain that Bret Harte must have met him at least on several occasions. Mr. Neal stated that up to the time of the Midwinter Fair, the output of gold from Tuolumne county reached the astonishing figures of $250,000,000! What it has amounted to since that time, I had no means of ascertaining.

It is only twelve miles from Sonora to Tuolumne. From the top of the divide which separates the valleys there is a beautiful view of the surrounding country, the dim blue peaks of the Sierra Nevada forming the eastern sky-line. One of the chief charms of an excursion through these foothill counties is the certainty that directly you reach any considerable elevation there will be revealed a magnificent panorama, bounded only by the limit of vision, range after range of mountains running up in varying shades of blue and purple, to the far distant summits that indicate the backbone of California.

Tuolumne is situated in a circular basin rather than in a valley, and thus being protected from the wind, in hot weather the heat is intense. If there are any mining operations in the immediate vicinity, they are not in evidence to the casual observer. It is, however, one of the biggest timber camps in the State. In the yards of the West Side Lumber Company, covering several hundred acres, are stacked something like 30,000,000 feet of sugar pine. The logs are brought from the mountains twenty to twenty-five miles by rail, and sawn into lumber at Tuolumne. I was told that the bulk of the lumber manufactured here was shipped abroad, a great deal going to Australia.

Tuolumne, in Bret Harte's time, was called Summersville. It was destroyed by fire about fourteen years ago, but the new town has already so assimilated itself to the atmosphere of its surroundings, that its comparative youth might easily escape detection. Altogether, I was disappointed with Tuolumne, having expected to find a second Angel's, owing to its prominence in Bret Harte's stories. A lumber camp, while an excellent thing in its way, is neither picturesque nor inspiring. I spent the night at the "Turnback Inn," a large frame building, handsomely finished interiorly and built since the fire. It is, I believe, quite a summer resort, as Tuolumne is the terminus of the Sierra Railway, and one can go by way of Stockton direct to Oakland and San Francisco.

Returning to Angel's the next day, I lingered again at Tuttletown. There is a strange attraction about the place--it would hold you apart from its associations,

The old hotel, fast going to decay, surrounded by splendid trees whose shade is so dense as to be impenetrable to the noon-day sun, is a study for an artist. And as I gazed in a sort of day-dream at the ruins of what once was one of the liveliest camps in the Sierras--with four faro tables running day and night--the pines seemed to whisper a sigh of regret over its departed glories. Jackass Hill is fairly honeycombed with prospect holes, shafts and tunnels. I was surprised to see that even now there is a certain amount of prospect work going forward, for I noticed several shafts with windlasses to which ropes were attached; and, in fact, was told that the old camp showed signs of a new lease of life.

Musing on Tuttletown and its environment later on got me into serious difficulty. Having crossed the Stanislaus River and cleared the canon, I abandoned the main road for an alleged "cut-off." This I was following with the utmost confidence, when, to my surprise, it came to an abrupt end at the foot of a steep hill. In the ravine below was a house, and there fortunately I found a man of whom I inquired if I was in "Carson Flat." "Carson Flat? Well, I should say not! You're 'way off!" "How much?" I asked feebly. "Oh, several miles." This in a tone that implied that though I was in a bad fix, it might possibly be worse. However, with the invariable kindness of these people, he put me on a trail which, winding up to the summit of a ridge, struck down into Carson Flat and joined the main road. And there I registered a vow: "The hard highway for me!" As a consequence of this deviation, I materially lengthened the distance to Angel's. It is thirty miles from Tuolumne by the road, to which, by taking the "cut-off," I probably added another three!

It is surprising how these towns grow upon one. Already the Angel's Hotel seemed like home to me and after an excellent dinner, I joined the loungers on the side-walk and became one of a row, seated on chairs tilted at various angles against the wall of the hotel. And there I dozed, watching the passing show between dreams; for in the evening when the electric lights are on, there is a sort of parade of the youth and beauty of the town, up and down the winding street.

On account of the great heat that even the dry purity of the Sierra atmosphere could not altogether mitigate, I decided the next day to be content with reaching San Andreas, the county seat of Calaveras County, fifteen miles north of Angel's.

Apart from its name, there is something about San Andreas that suggests Mexico, or one's idea of pastoral California in the early days of the American occupation.

The streets are narrow and unpaved and during the midday heat are almost deserted. Business of some sort there must be, for the little town, though somnolent, is evidently holding its own; but there seems to be infinite time in which to accomplish whatever the necessities of life demand. And I may state here parenthetically, that perhaps the most impressive feature of all the old California mining towns is their suggestion of calm repose. Each little community seems sufficient unto itself and entirely satisfied with things as they are. Not even in the Old World will you find places where the current of life more placidly flows.

On the main street--and the principal street of all these towns is "Main Street"--I had the good fortune to be introduced to Judge Ira H. Reed, who came to Calaveras County in 1854, and has lived there ever since. He told me that Judge Gottschalk, who died a few years ago at an advanced age, was authority for the statement that Mark Twain got his "Jumping Frog" story from the then proprietor of the Metropolitan Hotel, San Andreas, who asserted that the incident actually occurred in his bar-room. Twain, it is true, places the scene in a bar-room at Angel's, but that is doubtless the author's license. Bret Harte calls Tuttletown, "Tuttleville," and there never was a "Wingdam" stage.

That evening as I lay awake in my bedroom at the Metropolitan Hotel, wondering by what person of note it had been occupied in the "good old days," my attention was attracted to the musical tinkle of a cow-bell. Looking out of the window, I beheld the strange spectacle of a cow walking sedately down the middle of the street. No one was driving her, no one paid her any attention beyond a casual glance, as she passed. The cow, in fact, had simply come home, after a day in the open country; and it became plain to me that this was a nightly occurrence and therefore caused no comment. Unmolested, she passed the hotel and on down the street to the foot of the hill, where she evidently spent the night; for the tinkle of the bell became permanent and blended with and became a part of the subtle, mysterious sounds that constitute Nature's sleeping breath.

This little incident in the county seat of Calaveras County impressed me as an epitome of the changes wrought by time, since the days when in song and story Bret Harte made the name "Calaveras" a synonym for romance wherever the English language is spoken.

From San Andreas my objective point was Placerville, distant about forty-five miles. The heat still being excessive, I made the town by easy stages, arriving at noon on the third day. Mokelumne Hill, ten miles beyond San Andreas, also lends its name to the little town which clusters around its apex and is at the head of Chili Gulch, a once famous bonanza for the placer miners. For miles the road winds up the gulch, which is almost devoid of timber, amid piled-up rocks and debris, bleached and blistered by the sun's fierce rays; the gulch itself being literally stripped to "bedrock." I had already witnessed many evidences of man's eager pursuit of the precious metal, but nothing that so conveyed the idea of the feverish, persistent energy with which those adventurers in the new El Dorado had struggled day and night with Nature's obstacles, spurred on by the auri sacra fames.

A little incident served to relieve the monotony of the climb up Chili Gulch. A miner, who might have sat for a study of "Tennessee's Partner," came down the hillside with a pan of "dirt," which he carefully washed in a muddy pool in the bed of the gulch. He showed me the result, a few "colors" and sulphurets. He said it would "go about five dollars to the ton," and seemed well satisfied with the result. I shall always hold him in grateful memory, for he took me to an old tunnel, and disappearing for a few moments, returned with a large dipper of ice-cold water. Not the Children of Israel, when Aaron smote the rock in the desert and produced a living stream, could have lapped that water with keener enjoyment.

The terrific heat in Chili Gulch made the shade from the trees which surround Mekolumne Hotel doubly grateful. Mokelumne Hill is, in fact, a mountain, and commands a view of rare beauty. At its base winds the wooded canon of the Mokelumne River, on the farther side of which rises the Jackson Butte, an isolated peak with an elevation of over three thousand feet, while in the background loom the omnipresent peaks of the far Sierra.

The Mokelumne Hotel is regarded as modern, dating back merely to 1868, at which time the original building was destroyed by fire. The present structure of solid blocks of stone, should resist the elements for centuries to come. I was surprised at the excellent accommodations of this hotel. In what seemed such an out-of-the-way and inaccessible locality, I was served with one of the best meals on the whole journey, including claret with crushed ice in a champagne glass! What that meant to a tramp who had struggled for miles through quartz rock and impalpable dust, up a heavy grade, without shade and the thermometer well past the hundred mark, only a tramp can appreciate. I fell in love with Mokelumne Hill and, after due consultation of my map, resolved to pass the night in this picturesque and delightful spot. I was also influenced by its associations, as it figures prominently in Bret Harte's stories.

Of the four famous rivers--the Stanislaus, Mokelumne, American and Cosumnes--which I crossed on this trip, the Mokelumne appealed to me the most. Whatever the meaning of the Indian name, one may rest assured it stands for some form of beauty. Jackson, the county seat of Amador County, is but six miles from Mokelumne Hill and a town of considerable importance, being the terminus of a branch line of the Southern Pacific Railway. It is situated in an open country where the hills are at some distance, and presents a certain up-to-date appearance. About a mile from Jackson the Kennedy mine, running a hundred stamps, is one of the greatest gold producers in the State.

Sutter Creek, erroneously supposed by many to be the spot where gold was first discovered in California, four miles north of Jackson, is picturesque and rendered attractive by reason of the vivid green of the lawns surrounding the little cottages on its outskirts. This town, too, has a flourishing look, accounted for by the operation of the South Eureka and Central Eureka mines. A gentleman whom I met on the street imparted this information, and asked me if I remembered Mark Twain's definition of a gold mine. I had to confess I did not. "Well," said he, "Mark Twain defined a gold mine as 'a hole in the ground at one end, and a d--d fool at the other!'" The appreciative twinkle in his eye suggested the possibility that this definition met with his approval.

Amador, two miles beyond Sutter Creek, did not appeal to me. "Stagnation" would probably come nearer than any other term to conveying to the mind of a person unfamiliar with Amador its present condition. One becomes acutely sensitive to the "atmosphere" of these places, after a few days upon the road, for each has a distinctive individuality. in spite of the fact that it was mid-day in midsummer, gloom seemed to pervade the streets and to be characteristic of its inhabitants. With the exception of an attempt to get into telephonic communication with a friend at Placerville, I lost not a moment in the town.

On reaching Drytown, three miles north of Amador, I noted the thermometer stood at 110 degrees in the shade on the watered porch of the hotel, and deciding there was a certain risk attendant on walking in such heat, determined to make the best of what was anything but a pleasant situation, and go no farther. Drytown, in the modern application of the first syllable, is a misnomer, the "town" consisting chiefly of the hotel with accompanying bar, and a saloon across the way!

Drytown was in existence as early as 1849, and was visited in October of that year by Bayard Taylor. He says: "I found a population of from two to three hundred, established for the winter. The village was laid out with some regularity and had taverns, stores, butchers' shops and monte tables." One cannot but smile at the idea of "monte tables" in connection with the Drytown of to-day; pitiful as is the reflection that men had braved the hardships of the desert and toiled to the waist in water for gold, only to throw it recklessly in the laps of professional gamblers.

The Exchange Hotel, a wooden building dating back to 1858, stands on the site of the original hotel, built in 1851 and burned in 1857. Upon the front porch is a well furnishing cold, pure water. I found this to be the most acceptable feature of several of the old hostelries. The well and the swinging sign over the entrance suggested the wayside inn of rural England; more especially as the surrounding country carries out the idea, being gently undulating and well timbered.

The following evening I put up at Nashville, on the North Fork of the Cosumnes River and well over the borders of El Dorado county, passing Plymouth en route. Plymouth, on the map, appeared to be a place of some importance, but a closer inspection proved that--in spite of its breezy name--it would take the spirits of a Mark Tapley to withstand its discouraging surroundings. Plymouth is "living in hopes," an English syndicate having an option on certain mining properties in the vicinity; but Nashville is frankly "out of business."

At Nashville, in fact, I had some difficulty in securing "bed and lodging." There appeared to be only three families in this once flourishing camp. Strange as it may seem, money appears to be no object to people in these sequestered places. You have "to make good," and in this instance it required not a little tact and diplomacy.

I arrived at Placerville the following day. Due to taking a road not shown on my map, I went several miles astray and for some few hours was immersed in wild, chaparral-covered mountains, with evidences on all hands of deserted mines; finally crossing a divide at an elevation of two thousand feet and descending into the valley where slumbers the little town of El Dorado, formerly bearing the less attractive designation "Mud Springs." This title, though lacking in euphony, was more in keeping with actual conditions, since the valley is noted for its springs, and Diamond Springs, a mile or two north, is quite a summer resort. Nor is there any indication of the precious metal anywhere in the immediate vicinity.

In Placerville--known as "Hangtown" in the Bret Harte days--I registered at the Cary House, which once had the honor of entertaining no less a personage than Horace Greeley. It was here he terminated his celebrated stage ride with Hank Monk. I found that my friend Harold Edward Smith had gone to Coloma, eight miles on the road to Auburn, and had left a note saying he would wait for me there the following morning.

Chapter IV
J. H. Bradley and the Cary House. Ruins of Coloma. James W. Marshall and His Pathetic End.

More than any other town, Placerville gave a suggestion of the olden times. "John Oakhurst" and "Jack Hamlin" would still be in their element, as witness the following scene:

In the card room back of the bar, in a certain hotel, a "little game" was in progress. A big, blond giant, with curly hair and clean-cut features--indeed he could have posed as a model for Praxiteles--arose nonchalantly from the table as I entered, and swept the stakes into a capacious pocket. An angry murmur of disapproval came from the sitters, and one man muttered something about "quitting the game a winner." With a hand on each hip, the giant swept the disgruntled upturned faces with a comprehensive glance, and drawled: "I'll admit there's something wrong in mine, gentlemen, or I wouldn't be here, see?" He waited a moment and amid silence passed slowly through the barroom to the sidewalk, seated himself, stretched his long legs and placidly gazed across the street.

In the morning I had a long talk with Mr. J. H. Bradley, perhaps the best known man in El Dorado County. Though in his eighty-fourth year, his keen brown eyes still retain the fire and light of youth. The vitality of these old pioneers is something marvelous. Mr. Bradley was born in Kentucky, but, as a boy, moved to Hannibal, Missouri, where he played marbles with Mark Twain, or Clemens, as he prefers to call him. In '49, he came across the plains to California. He was on the most friendly terms with Twain and said he assisted him to learn piloting on the Mississippi; and when Twain came to California, helped him to get a position as compositor with U. E. Hicks, who founded the Sacramento Union. He also knew Horace Greeley intimately, and has a portfolio that once was his property. Five years after Greeley's arrival in Placerville, which was in 1859, Mr. Bradley married Caroline Hicks, who with Phoebe and Rose Carey had acted as secretary to Mr. Greeley. Mr. Bradley takes no stock in the "keep your seat, Horace!" story. He considers it a fabrication. In his opinion, the romancers--Bret Harte, Mark Twain, et al.--have done California more harm than good. He also has a thinly disguised contempt for "newspaper fellows and magazine writers." Nor does he believe in the "Mother Lode"--that is, in its continuity--in spite of the geologists. He prefers to speak of the "mineral zone." In fine, Mr. Bradley is a man of definite and pronounced opinions on any subject you may broach. For that reason, his views, whether you agree with them or not, are always of interest.

Hanging in the office of the Cary House is a clever cartoon, by William Cooper, of Portland, Oregon, entitled "A mining convention in Placerville;" in which Mr. Bradley is depicted in earnest conversation with a second Mr. Bradley, a third and evidently remonstrant Mr. Bradley intervening, while a fourth and fifth Mr. Bradley, decidedly bored, are hurriedly departing.

Indeed, one glance at Mr. Bradley is enough to convince you that he is a man of unusual force of character. No one introduced me to him. I was merely informed at the Cary House that he was the person to whom I should apply for information concerning the old times. I accordingly started out to look for him and had not proceeded fifty yards when a man, approaching at a distance, arrested my attention. As he drew nearer, I felt positive there could be only one such personage in Placerville, and when he was opposite me, I stopped and said, "How are you, Mr. Bradley?" "That's my name, sir; what do you want?" he replied.

They take life easily in the old mining towns. No wonder the spectacle of a man with a pack on his back caused comment, in that heat, tramping two or three hundred miles for pleasure! Beyond the trivial necessities that bare existence makes imperative, I was not conscious of seeing anyone do anything on the whole trip. Old miners not unnaturally took me for a prospector, and I think I never quite succeeded in convincing them to the contrary.

In Placerville as in Angel's Camp, the evening promenade seems the most important event of the day. Young men and maidens pass and repass in an apparently endless chain. The same faces recur so frequently that one begins to take an interest in the little comedy and speculate on the rival attractions of blonde and brunette, and wonder which of the young bloods is the local Beau Brummel. The audience--so to speak--sit on, chairs backed against the walls of the hotels and stores, while many prefer the street itself, and with feet on curb or other coign of vantage, tilt their chairs at most alarming angles. A sort of animated lovers' lane is thus formed, through which the promenaders have to run the gauntlet, and are subjected to a certain amount of criticism. Everyone knows everyone. Good natured badinage plays like wild-fire, up and down and across the street. Later on, the tinkle of mandolin and guitar is heard far into the night watches.

Having determined to reach Auburn--thirty miles away--the next day, I made an early start. Coloma lies at the bottom of the great canon of the South Fork of the American River. Hastening down the grade, in a bend of the road I almost ran into my friend. It seemed a strange meeting this, in the heart of the old mining country, and I think we both gave a perceptible start.

It was at Coloma that gold was first discovered in California, by James W. Marshall, January 19, 1848. My companion had been so fortunate on the previous day as to meet Mr. W. H. Hooper, who arrived in Coloma August 8, 1850, and who has lived there practically ever since. Though eighty-three, he is still strong and vigorous. From him my friend elicited some very interesting information in regard to Marshall especially, the substance of which I append from his notes. Mr. Hooper had known Marshall for many years, and his reminiscences of the discoverer have a touch of pathos bordering on the tragic.

Marshall, a trapper by trade and frontiersman by inclination, accompanied General Sutter to California, assisted in the building of Sutter Fort and, on account of his mechanical ability, was sent to Coloma to superintend the erection of a sawmill. It was in the mill-race that he picked up the nugget which made the name "California" the magnet for the world's adventurers. Unaware of the nature of his "find," he took it to Sacramento, where it was declared to be gold. He was implored by General Sutter to keep the mill operatives in ignorance of his discovery, for fear they should desert their work. But how could such a secret be kept, especially by a man of generous and impulsive instincts? At any rate the news leaked out and the stampede followed.

From Mr. Hooper's account, Marshall was a very human character. Late in life the state legislature granted him a pension of two hundred dollars per month. This sum being far in excess of his actual needs, it followed as a matter of course that his cronies assisted him in disposing of it. In fact, "Marshall's pension day" became a local attraction, and the Coloma saloon--still in existence--the rendezvous. These reunions were varied by glorious excursions to Sacramento, his friends in the legislature imploring him to keep away. After two years the pension was cut down to one hundred dollars per mouth and finally was discontinued in toto--a shabby and most undignified procedure. Opposite the saloon, at some little distance, is a conical hill. For many years Marshall, seated on the steps of the porch, had gazed dreamily at its summit. Shortly before his death, addressing a remnant of the "old guard," he exclaimed: "Boys, when I go, I want you to plant me on the top of that hill." And "planted" he was, with a ten-thousand-dollar monument on top of him!

The poor old fellow died in poverty at Kelsey, near Coloma, August 10, 1885, at the age of seventy-five. It is a sad reflection that a tithe of the money spent on the monument would have comforted him in his latter days; for the blow to his pride by the withdrawal of his pension, still more than the actual lack of funds, hastened the end.

Mr. Hooper intimated that the population of Coloma diminished perceptibly after the termination of Marshall's pension. In common with the majority of the old miners, he saved nothing and never profited to any extent by the discovery that will keep his memory alive for centuries to come.

Coloma in its palmy days had a population variously estimated at from five to ten thousand souls, with the usual accompaniment of saloons, dance halls and faro banks. There was a vigorous expulsion of gamblers in the early fifties and an incident occurred which quite possibly supplied the inspiration for Bret Harte's "Outcasts of Poker Flat." A notorious gambler and desperado, and his accomplice, demurred. Whereupon the irate miners placed them on a burro, and with vigorous threats punctuated by a salvo of revolver shots fired over their heads, drove them out of camp. They disappeared over the hill upon which the monument now stands, and were seen no more.

Coloma suffered severely from fires. Little of the old town remains but ruins of stone walls, and here and there an isolated wooden building. The ruins, however, are not only exceedingly picturesque, being half buried in foilage of beautiful trees, but hold the imagination with a grip that is indescribable. I could willingly have tarried here for days.

But while old Coloma is dead, there is a new Coloma that furnishes an extraordinary contrast. It is a sweet and peaceful little hamlet, situated on the lower benches of the canon, well up out of the river bottom, and is entirely devoted to horticulture. One has read of birds building their nests in the muzzles of old and disused cannon; even that does not suggest a more anomalous association of ideas than the spectacle of a vine-clad cottage shaded by fig trees, basking peacefully in the sun, so close to what was at one time a veritable maelstrom of human passions. So far as the new Coloma is concerned, Marshall's discovery might never have been made. Nowhere else will you find a spot where gold and what it stands for would seem to mean so little, Coloma! It is passing strange that a name so sweet and restful should forever be linked with the wildest scramble for gold the world has ever seen!

Chapter V
Auburn to Nevada City Via Colfax and Grass Valley. Ben Taylor and His Home

After surmounting the canon of the South Fork of the American River, you gradually enter a open country, the outskirts of the great deciduous fruit belt in Placer County, which supplies New York and Chicago with choice plums, peaches and pears. About three miles from Auburn, the road plunges into one of the deepest canons of the Sierras, at the bottom of which the Middle and North Forks of the American River unite. Just below the junction, the river is spanned by a long suspension bridge. Auburn is remarkably situated in that one sees nothing of it until the rim of the canon is reached, at least a thousand feet above the river. Thus there are no outskirts and you plunge at once into the business streets, passing the station of the Central Pacific Railway, which line skirts the edge of the canon on a heavy grade.

I had accomplished a good thirty miles but that did not prevent me from accompanying my friend on a long and protracted hunt for comfortable quarters in which to eat and spend the night. There was quite an attractive hotel near the railroad, but actuated by a desire to see something of the town, which we found to be more than usually drawn out, we passed it with lingering regret. Whether by chance or instinct, we drifted to the ruins of the old hotel, now in process of reconstruction, and were comfortably housed in a wooden annex.

Auburn marks the western verge of the mineral zone, but in the fifties there were, rich placer diggings in the immediate vicinity. There are some remarkably solid buildings of that period, in the old portion of the town, which, as customary, is situated in the bottom of the winding valley or ravine. Practically a new town, called "East Auburn," has been started on higher ground, and a fight is on to move the post office; but the people in the hollow having the voting strength, hang on to it like grim death. Along the edge of the American River canon and commanding a magnificent view, are the homes of the local aristocracy. In christening Auburn, it is scarcely credible that the pioneers had in mind Goldsmith's "loveliest village of the Plain;" nor, keeping the old town in view, is the title remarkably applicable today.

Our next objective point being Colfax, distant in a north-easterly direction only fifteen miles, we made a leisurely inspection of the town and vicinity in the morning. The old town proved of absorbing interest to my friend, and we became separated while he was hunting up subjects for the camera. Having a free and easy working scheme in such matters, after a few minutes' search, I gave up the quest and started alone on the road to Colfax.

A few miles out, I met a man with a rifle on his shoulder, leading a burro bearing a pack-saddle laden in the most scientific manner with probably all his worldly possessions, the pick and shovel plainly denoting a prospector. A water bucket on one side of the animal was so adjusted that the bottom was uppermost; on the top of the bucket sat a little fox-terrier, his eyes fixed steadfastly on his master. I paused a moment, possessed with a strong desire to take a snap shot of this remarkable equipment, but the man with the gun gave me a glance that settled the matter. His was not a bad face--far from it--but the features were stern and set, the cheeks furrowed with deep lines that bespoke hardship and fatigue in the struggle with Nature and the elements. That glance out of the tail of his eye meant: "Let me alone and I will let you alone, but let me alone!"

Taciturnity becomes habitual to men accustomed to vast solitudes. Even on such a tramp as I had undertaken, in which I frequently walked for miles without sight or sound of a human being, I began to realize how banal and aimless is conventional conversation. Under such conditions you feel yourself in sympathy with the man who says nothing unless he has something to say, and who, in turn, expects the same restriction of speech from you.

I was seated on the porch of the store at Applegate, disposing of a frugal lunch consisting of raisins and crackers, when my friend hove in sight. After a private inspection of the store's possibilities, with a little smile, the meaning of which I well understood from many similar experiences, he sat down beside me and without a word tackled the somewhat uninviting repast, to which with a wave of the hand I invited him. I may say here that Mr. Smith is a veteran and inveterate "hiker." I doubt very much whether any man in California has seen as much of this magnificent State as he, certainly not on foot; as a consequence he is accustomed to a ready acceptance of things as they are. Applegate, about midway between Auburn and Colfax, is an alleged "summer resort." It did not appeal to us as especially attractive, the view, at any rate from the road, being extremely limited and lacking any distinctive features. Without unnecessary delay, therefore, we resumed the march.

It is practically up-hill--"on the collar"--all the way to Colfax, as is plainly evidenced by the heavy railroad grade. About a mile short of the town, we made a digression to an Italian vineyard of note. There, at a long table under a vine-covered trellis that connected the stone cellar with the dwelling-house, we were served with wine by a young woman having the true Madonna features of Sunny Italy, her mother, a comely matron, in the meantime preparing the evening meal, while on the hard ground encumbered with no superfluous clothing, disported the younger members of the family. And as I sat and smoked the pipe of peace, I reflected upon how much better they do these things in Italy--for to all intents and Purposes, I was in Italy.

Colfax--before the advent of the C. P. R. R. called "Illinois Town"--is an odd blending of past and present; the solid structures of the mining days contrasting strangely with the flimsy wooden buildings that seem to mark a railroad town. We were amazed at the amount of traffic that occurs in the night. Three big overland trains passed through in either direction, the interim being filled in with the switching of cars, accompanied apparently with a most unnecessary ringing of bells and piercing shrieks from whistles. Since our hotel was not more than a hundred and fifty feet from the main line, with no intervening buildings to temper the noises, sleep of any consequence was an utter impossibility.

Few Californians are aware, probably, that a considerable amount of tobacco is raised in the foothills of the Sierras. At Colfax, I smoked a very fair cigar made from tobacco grown in the vicinity, and manufactured in the town.

I think we were both glad to leave Colfax. Apart from a nerve-racking night, the mere proximity of the railroad with its accompanying associations served constantly to bring to mind all that I had fled to the mountains to escape. Yet I cannot bring myself to agree with those who profess to brand a railroad "a blot on the landscape." The enormous engines which pull the overland trains up the heavy grades of the Sierra Nevada impress one by their size, strength and suggestion of reserve power, as not being out of harmony with the forces of Nature they are constructed to contend with and overcome.

This thought occurred to us as we watched a passenger train slowly winding its way around the famous Cape Horn, some four miles from Colfax. Although several miles in an air line intervened, one seemed to feel the vibrations in the air caused by the panting monster, while great jets of steam shot up above the pine trees. I confess to a sense of elation at the spectacle. Nature in some of her moods seems so malignant, that I felt proud of this magnificent exhibition of man's victory over the obstacles she so well knows how to interpose.

The road between Colfax and Grass Valley--the next stopping place on our itinerary--lay through so lovely a country that we passed through it as in a dream. Descending into the valley we were joined by several small boys, attracted, I suppose, by our--to them--unusual costume and equipment, who plied us with questions. They asked if "we carried a message for the mayor," and were visibly disappointed when we regretted we had overlooked that formality. For several minutes they kept us busy trying to give truthful answers to most unexpected questions. They had never heard of Tuolumne and wanted to know if it was in California. Their world, in fact, was bounded by Colfax on the south and Nevada City on the north.

Grass Valley received its name from the meadow in which the town, for the most part, is situated. The ground is so moist that, notwithstanding the heat, the grass was a vivid green. Apple trees growing in the grass, as in the orchards of England and in the Atlantic States, and perfectly healthy, conveyed that suggestion of the Old World which lends a peculiar charm to these towns. And Grass Valley really is a town, having seven thousand inhabitants; and is, withal, clean, picturesque and altogether delightful. One understood why "Tuolumne" sounded meaningless to those small boys. Thus early in life they were under influences which will probably keep them in after years--as they kept their fathers--permanent citizens of the town of Grass Valley.

Grass Valley was one of the richest of the old mining camps. There was literally gold everywhere, even in the very roots of the grass. The mining is now all underground and drifts from the North Star and Ophir mines underlie a part of the town.

After a methodical search, we discovered an excellent restaurant and made a note of it as a recurrent possibility. A judicious choice of a suitable place in which to eat and eke, to pass the night, is to the tramp a matter of vital interest. Robert Louis Stevenson, in those entertaining narratives "An Inland Voyage" and "Travels with a Donkey," lays heartfelt stress on these particulars; when things were not to his liking, roundly denouncing them, but if agreeably surprised, lifting up his voice in song and praise.

Though tempted to pass the night in Grass Valley, impelled by curiosity, we pushed on four miles farther, to Nevada City. It is useless to attempt to convey in words the fascination of Nevada City. My friend, who is familiar with the country, said it reminded him of Italy. Houses rise one above the other on the hillside; while down below, the winding streets with their quaint old-time stores and balconied windows, are equally attractive. The horrors of the previous night at Colfax made the quiet peacefulness of Nevada City the more refreshing. At the National Hotel I enjoyed the soundest sleep since leaving home.

In the morning there was a delicious breeze from the mountains, which rendered strolling about the town a pleasure. According to custom, we went our several ways, each drawn by what appealed to him the most at the moment. When ready to depart, finding no trace of my companion at the hotel, I left word that I had returned to Grass Valley; where an hour or two later, he rejoined me.

More fortunate than I, my friend by chance encountered Mr. Morrison M. Green, on the street in front of his home upon the hill which looks down upon the town. This gentleman, who is in his eighty-third year, related an almost incredible incident in connection with the fire in 1857, which wiped out the town, with the exception of one house. Three prominent citizens who chanced to have met in a saloon when the fire broke out, having the utmost confidence in the safety of a certain building, on account of its massive walls and iron door, made a vow to lock themselves in it, and actually did so. They might perhaps have withstood the ordeal, had not the roof been broken in by the fall of the walls of the adjoining building. The iron door having been warped with the heat, it was impossible to open it; when last seen, they were standing with their arms around one another in the center of the store.

At Grass Valley, my friend--greatly to my regret and I think also to his own--received word which rendered his return to San Francisco imperative. After a farewell dinner at the restaurant before mentioned, I accompanied him to the railway station, and in the words of Christian in "The Pilgrim's Progress," "I saw him no more in my dream." I confess to a feeling of depression after his departure, for however enjoyable the experiences of the road, they are rendered doubly so by the sympathetic companionship of a man endowed not only with a keen sense of humor but also with an unusual perception of human nature.

After registering at the Holbrooke--a substantial survival of the old times--I called by appointment on Mr. Ben Taylor, a much respected citizen of Grass Valley and probably the oldest inhabitant of Nevada County, having reached the patriarchal age of eighty-six.

Mr. Taylor has a charming home with extensive grounds overlooking the town and surrounding country. In his garden is a spruce he planted himself forty-five years ago, and apple trees of the same age. The spruce now has the appearance of a forest tree and shades the whole front of the house. His present home was built in 1864 and from all appearances should last the century out. He said the lumber was carefully selected, the boards being heavier than usual, and all the important timbers, instead of being nailed, were morticed and dove-tailed. This thoroughness of workmanship accounts for the excellent condition of the wooden buildings in these towns, many of which were constructed over fifty years ago.

Mr. Taylor came to Grass Valley September 22, 1849, and has lived there almost continuously ever since. He crossed the plains one of twenty-five men, the last of his companions dying in 1905. The little band suffered many hardships, having to be constantly on watch for Indians, though he said they were more fearful of the Mormons. They came over the old emigrant trail across the Sierra Nevada. When they reached Grass Valley, their Captain, a man named Broughton, exclaimed: "Boys! here's the gold; this is good enough for us!" And there they stayed, the twenty-five of them!

Mr. Taylor had frequently met Mark Twain, but never to his knowledge, Bret Harte. In common with other men who had known the Great American Humorist, Mr. Taylor smiled at the bare mention of his name. Twain's breezy, hail-fellow-well-met manner, combined with his dry humor, insured him a welcome at all the camps; he was a man who would "pass the time of day" and take a friendly drink with any man upon the road. Twain, he told me, and a man with whom he was traveling on one occasion, lost their mules. They tracked them to a creek and concluding the mules had crossed it, Twain said to his companion: "What's the use of both of us getting wet? I'll carry you!" The other complying, Twain reached in safety the deepest part of the creek and, purposely or not, dropped him. A man, to play such pranks as this, must be sure of his standing in a primitive community.

Mr. Taylor is known to everyone in Nevada County as "Ben." His genial manner and kindly nature are apparent at a glance. But while Ben Taylor was on friendly terms with Mark Twain, he was never so intimate with him as with Bayard Taylor, whom, it seems, he much resembled. This accidental likeness, combined with the similarity of names, caused many more or less amusing but embarrassing complications, since they were frequently taken for each other and received each other's correspondence.

I asked Ben Taylor--he rightly dislikes "Mister," perhaps the ugliest and most inappropriate word in the English language--if the shootings and hangings which figure so prominently in the stories of the romancers were not exaggerations. He said he certainly was of that opinion. I said: "As a matter of fact, did you ever see a man either shot or hung for a crime?" "I never did," he replied with emphasis. "But I once came across the bodies of several men who had been strung up for horse-stealing; that, however, was not in Grass Valley."

Ben Taylor was present when Lola Montez horsewhipped Henry Shibley, editor of the Grass Valley National, for what she considered derogatory reflections on herself, published in his paper. It can readily be understood that Grass Valley was at that time a place of importance, when Lola Montez considered it worth while to stay there several years and sing and dance for the miners.

In parting, Ben Taylor told me pathetically that his wife had died a few years before and he had never recovered from the blow; "I am merely marking time until the end comes," he added. Since his married daughter and family live with him, he is assured in his latter days of loving care and attention.

Chapter VI
E. W. Maslin and His Recollections of Pioneer Days In Grass Valley. Origin of Our Mining Laws

To Mr. E. W. Maslin, of Alameda, of whom Ben Taylor said: "He is like a brother to me," I am indebted for information of much interest, bearing on the olden days and Grass Valley in particular. Mr. Maslin came around the "Horn" to California, in the ship Herman, on May 7, 1853. He arrived in Grass Valley and went to work as a miner the following morning. He now holds, and has for years, the responsible position in the United States Custom House, San Francisco, of Deputy Naval Officer of the Port. The clearing papers of every vessel that leaves San Francisco bear his signature. Although in his eightieth year, his memory is as clear and his sense of humor as vivid as when, a youth of nineteen, he left for good, Maryland, his native state. Few men in the San Francisco bay region are more widely known than he. His ready wit, cheery laugh and fund of information--for he is extremely well-read--always insure for him an attentive and appreciative audience.

Speaking of Ben Taylor, he told me a characteristic incident, which being also typical of the men of '49, I give, with his consent, as related. When the White Pine excitement in 1869 started a rush of prospectors to Nevada, Mr. Maslin caught the fever with the rest. In common with all who dug for gold, he had his ups and downs, the fat years and the lean ones; at the time, his fortunes being at a lew ebb, he joined the stampede. Several years previous to his departure, without informing his wife, he had borrowed of Ben Taylor, three hundred dollars, secured by mortgage on his house in Grass Valley. At White Pine he met with considerable success, and in a short time sent his wife five hundred dollars, telling her for the first time of the mortgage on their home and requesting her to go to Ben Taylor at once and pay him in full. It so happened that Taylor had called on Mrs. Maslin for news of her husband, as she was reading this letter. She immediately tendered him the check with the request that he would inform her to what the interest amounted. "Why, Molly," said Ben Taylor, "you surely ought to know me well enough to know I would never take any interest on that money!" When it is remembered that the legal rate of interest at that time was ten per cent, and that double that amount was not infrequently paid--Mr. Maslin, in fact, expecting to pay Taylor something like five hundred dollars--the attitude of the latter will be the better appreciated.

This seems a fitting place to pay a humble personal tribute of respect to the memory of the men of "the fall of '49 and the spring of '50." Not since the Crusades, when the best blood of Europe was spilt in defense of the Holy Sepulchre, has the world seen a finer body of men than the Argonauts of California. True, the quest of the "Golden Fleece" was the prime motive, but sheer love of adventure for adventure's sake played a most important part. Later on, the turbulent element arrived. It was due to the rectitude, inherent sense of justice and courage of the pioneers that they were held in check and, by force of arms when necessary, made to understand the white man's code of honor.

So much in song and story has been said of the scramble for gold in the early days after the discovery, and so little attention given to the artistic and aesthetic sense of the pioneers, that the general impression made by the famous old mining towns of California, when seen for the first time, may be worth recording. In the massive stone hotels and stores of that period, as well as in the careful construction of dwelling houses, they exhibited a true perception of "the eternal fitness of things." The buildings of the fifties, in their extreme simplicity, are far more imposing than the nondescript, pretentious structures of today, and will, beyond doubt, in usefulness outlast them.

As a result of ignoring the checker-board plan, and permitting the streets to follow the natural contour of the hills and ravines, these mountain towns seem to have become blended and to be in harmony with the wonderful setting Nature has provided. All buildings, residential or otherwise, are protected from the summer heat by umbrageous trees. Lawns of richest green delight the eye, and vines and flowers surround cottages perched on steep hillsides, or half-hidden in deep ravines. The first glimpse from a distant eminence of any of the old mining towns conveys the suggestion of peaceful homes buried in greenery, basking contentedly in the brilliant sunshine, surrounded by the whispering pines, with the snow-clad peaks of the Sierra Nevada for a background.

You also receive the impression of cleanliness. If there were any old cans, scraps of paper and miscellaneous rubbish lying about in any town through which I passed, I did not notice them. One is struck, too, by the absence of the "vacant lot"--that unsightly blot of such frequent occurrence in all towns in the process of building, especially when forced by "booms" beyond their normal growth. Fortunately the very word "boom," in its significance as applied to inflated real estate values, has no meaning in these towns, with the result that they are compact. One may search in vain for the "house to let" sign. When no more houses were needed, no more houses were built. This compactness of form, cleanliness, and the elimination to a great extent of the rectangular block, contribute in no small measure to that indefinable suggestion of the Old World--a charm that haunts the memory and finally becomes permanent acquisition.

However clever the stories of the romancers--of whom Bret Harte preeminently stands first--after all, their characters were intrinsically but creatures of the imagination; the pioneers were the real thing! Yet such is the nature of this topsy-turvy world, the copies will remain, whilst the originals will fade away and be forgotten! The writer will always hold it a privilege that he had the pleasure of meeting in the flesh a remnant of the men who laid the foundation of the institutions by means of which this great Commonwealth has grown and prospered; big, broad-minded, strong men who, whatever their failings--for they were very human--were generous to a fault, ever ready to listen to the cry of distress or help a fallen brother to his feet, scornful of pettiness, ignorant of snobbery, fair and square in their dealings with their fellows. Alas, that it should have come to "Hail and Farewell" to such a type of manhood!

At my request, Mr. Maslin, at one time a practicing attorney, dictated the following succinct account of the origin of the mining laws of California. The discovery at Gold Hill, now within the corporate limits of Grass Valley, of a gold-bearing quartz ledge, subsequently the property of Englishmen who formed an organization known as "The Gold Hill Quartz Mining Company," led to the founding of the mining laws of California. On December 30, 1850, the miners passed regulations which had with them the force of laws, defining the location and ownership of mines. It was provided that claims should be forty feet by thirty feet; a recorder was to be elected by the miners and all difficulties arising out of trespass on claims were to be tried before the recorder and two miners, an appeal to be taken to the justice of the peace.

When quartz lodes began to be discovered and worked, it was found that the location of claims by square feet did not protect the miner or afford sufficient territory upon which to expend his labor. Accordingly a miners' meeting was held in Nevada City on December 20, 1852, and a body of laws prescribed, governing all quartz mines within the county of Nevada. The following were the salient features: "Each proprietor of a quartz claim shall be entitled to one hundred feet on a quartz ledge or vein; the discoverer shall be allowed one hundred feet additional. Each claim shall include all the dips, angles, and variations of the same." The remaining articles related to the working, holding and recording of claims. This law was incorporated in the raining legislation of the State of Nevada and has formed the basis of the mining laws of each territory of the United States. Thus we have a proof not only of the intelligence of the early miner, but also of his capacity for self-government. It must be remembered that the miners came from all over the United States, but principally from the West and the South. Probably none had seen a quartz ledge before coming to California, yet the necessity for extending a claim as far as the ledge dipped was soon perceived, as also the taking into consideration a change in the direction or course of the lode. Commenting on these laws and the causes leading to their adoption, Mr. Muslin became emphatic. He said:

"No body of rough, uncouth, pistolled ruffians, such as Bret Harte depicts the miners, would have formed such a group of benevolent, far-reaching and comprehensive laws. The early miner represented the best type of American character. He was brave, undeterred by obstacles, enduring with patient fortitude the perils and privations of the long journey of half a year by land, or a tempestuous voyage by sea; undaunted alike by the terrors of Cape Horn or the insidious diseases of the Isthmus of Panama. He met the, to him, hitherto unknown problem of the extraction of gold and solved it with the wisdom and vigor which distinguish the American. Observe that the provision against throwing dirt on another man's claim anticipated by many years the famous hydraulic decision of Judge Sawyer. It is another way of stating the maxim of law and equity: 'so use your own property, as not to injure that of another.'"

Mr. Maslin agrees with Ben Taylor that the hangings and shootings of the period following the discovery of gold have been grossly exaggerated. On this point he said: "I will venture to assert that in certain of the Mississippi Valley States, in their early settlement, more men were killed in one year than in ten of the early mining years in California." Of lynching, he said: "There were few lynchings in California, and those mostly in the southern tier of counties, of persons convicted of cattle-stealing." In connection with lynching he related a serio-comic incident that occurred in Grass Valley in the early days.

Several fires had taken place in the town and the inhabitants were in consequence much excited. A watchman on his rounds espied a light in a vacant log cabin, and entering, caught a man in the act of striking a match. He arrested him and the populace were for taking summary vengeance. A man known as "Blue Coat Osborne" cried out, "Let's hang him! Nevada City once hanged a man and Grass Valley never did!" This was an effective appeal, for the rivalry that has lasted ever since already existed. Fortunately, wiser counsels prevailed; the man was subsequently tried and acquitted, it appearing that he was a traveling prospector who had merely entered the cabin in order to light his pipe! In this connection, I may state that Mr. Maslin confirmed the story of the three friends in Nevada City, who attempted to withstand "the ordeal by fire."

Mr. Maslin is justly jealous for the reputation of the Argonauts. Perhaps Bret Harte's miner, with his ready pistol, was as far from the mark as Rudyard Kipling's picture of Tommy Atkins as "an absentminded beggar"--an imputation the real "Tommy" hotly resented. At the same time, such stories as "The Luck of Roaring Camp" and "Tennessee's Partner," not to quote others, prove Bret Harte conceded to the miner, courage, patience, gentleness, generosity and steadfastness in friendship. If Bret Harte really "hurt" California, it was because, leaving the State for good in February, 1871, he carried with him the atmosphere of the early mining days and never got out of it. He never realized the transition from mining to agriculture and horticulture, as the leading industries of the State. Thus his later stories which dealt with California, written long after the subsidence of the mining excitement, continued to convey to the Eastern or English reader an impression of the Californian as a bearded individual, his trousers tucked into long boots and the same old "red shirt" with the sleeves rolled back to the shoulders! As lately--comparatively speaking--as the Chicago Columbian Exposition, a lady told me she met at the Fair a woman who said she wanted to visit California, and asked if it would be safe to do so "on account of the Indians!" While Indians do not appear in Bret Harte's pages, it is a safe conjecture that, through association of ideas, this lady conjured up a vague vision of a "prairie schooner" crossing the plains, harassed by the Indian of the colored prints!

The following picture of the trying of a civil suit under difficulties, though in all probability causing little comment at the time, would undoubtedly do so at the present day, were the conditions possible. In 1853 Mr. Maslin owned, with his brother, a one-fifth interest in ten gravel claims at Pike Flat near Grass Valley. On the ground of alleged imperfection of location of a portion of these claims, they were "jumped," and litigation followed.

The case was called before "Si" Brown, a justice of the peace, at Rough and Ready, in a building (of which I obtained a photograph) used as a hotel and for other purposes. In the long room, now occupied as a store, Judge Brown held his court. On the right was a door leading to the bar. Extending the whole length of the room were four faro tables. At the rear the judge, jury, attorneys and the principals in the lawsuit made the best of the accommodations.

After stating the case, Judge Brown thus addressed the gamblers at the faro tables: "Boys, the court is now opened, call your games low!" In accordance with this request, though still audible, came in a monotonous undertone, the faro, dealers' oft-repeated call: "Gents, make your game--make your game!" The bets were put down and the cards called, in the same subdued voice. At intervals, an attorney on one side or the other would arise and say: "I move you, your Honor, that the court do now take a recess of ten minutes." The court: "The motion is sustained; but go softly, gentlemen, go softly!" It is probably needless to add that judge, jury, principals, attorneys and witnesses filed out of the door leading to the right; returning in ten minutes to resume the trial to the not altogether inappropriate accompaniment from the faro dealers, "Make your game, gents, make your game!"

The spirit of rivalry between Grass Valley and Nevada City has been accentuated, of late, by the efforts of the former town to secure the honor of being the county seat, on the claim that it possesses nearly double the population of Nevada City. Politics serve to intensify the feeling; Grass Valley, which contains many people of Southern birth, being largely Democratic in its affiliations, whilst Nevada City is as strongly, and, one may add, as conservatively, Republican.

Possibly the oldest building in Grass Valley is the Western Hotel. It is so hidden in the surrounding trees that it was with difficulty I took a photograph in which any portion of the hotel itself appeared. In the garden stands a splendid English walnut over forty years old; and on the porch, the well and pump to which I have before alluded as a distinguishing feature of the old-time hostelry, add a quaint and characteristic touch.

Grass Valley and Nevada City are nearly three thousand feet above sea level. The air, in consequence, is light and pure and the heat seldom excessive. It would be difficult, the world over, to find a more agreeable or salubrious climate.

It was with genuine regret that I left Grass Valley the following morning; not even Sonora possessed for me a stronger attraction. As I paused on the summit of the hill, for a farewell view of the town, I mentally resolved--the Fates permitting--I would pay another and more protracted visit to this land of enchantment.

Chapter VII
Grass Valley to Smartsville. Sucker Flat and its Personal Appeal.

I was heading due west for Smartsville, just across the line in Yuba County. In four miles, I came to Rough and Ready, once a famous camp. Save for the inevitable hotel, now used in part as a store, there was nothing to suggest the cause of its pristine glory or the origin of its emphatic designation; today it is simply a picturesque, rural hamlet. In Penn Valley, a mile or two farther on, I passed a smashed and abandoned automobile, the second wreck I had encountered. I thanked my star I traveled afoot; heavy going, it is true, in places, but safe and sure.

Notwithstanding the ubiquity of the autocar, it is still a fact that between the man in the car and the man on foot is set an impassable gulf. You are walking through a mountainous country, where every bend of the road reveals some new charm; absorbed in silent enjoyment of the scene, you have forgotten the very existence of the machine, when a raucous "honk" jolts you out of your daydream and causes you to jump for your life. In a swirl of dust the monster engulfs you, leaving you the dust and the stench of gasoline as souvenirs, but followed by your anathemas! This doubtless is where the man in the car thinks he has scored. Perhaps he has. When the dust on the road has settled and you have rubbed it out of your eyes, once more you forget his existence.

But the very speed with which he travels is the reason why the man in the car misses nearly all the charm of the country through which he is passing. On this tramp I took forty-odd photographs, all more or less of historical interest. Riding in an automobile, many of the subjects I would not have noticed or, if I had, I would not have been able to bring my camera into play. On several occasions I retraced my steps a good quarter of a mile, feeling I had lost a landscape, or street scene I might never again have the opportunity to behold.

What is of far greater consequence, the man on the road comes into touch not only with Nature, but the Children of Nature! In these days, automobiles are as thick as summer flies; you cannot escape them even in the Sierra foot-hills. No attention is paid them by the country people, unless they are in trouble or have caused trouble, which is mostly the case. But the man who "hikes" for pleasure is a source of perennial interest not unmixed with admiration, especially when walking with the thermometer indicating three figures in the shade. To him the small boy opens his heart; the "hobo" passes the time of day with a merry jest thrown in; the good housewife brings a glass of cold water or milk, adding womanlike, a little motherly advice; the passing teamster, or even stage-driver--that autocrat of the "ribbons"--shouts a cheery "How many miles today, Captain?" or, "Where did you start from this morning, Colonel?"--these titles perhaps due to the battered old coat of khaki.

All the humors of the road are yours. In fact, you yourself contribute to them, by your unexpected appearance on the scene and the novelty of your "make-up," if I may be pardoned the expression. At the hotel bar, you drink a glass of beer with the local celebrity and thus come into immediate touch with, the oldest inhabitant. After dinner, seated on a bench on the sidewalk, you smoke a pipe and discuss the affairs of the nation or of the town--usually the latter--with the man who in the morning offered to give you a lift and never will understand why you declined. Invariably you receive courteous replies and in kindly interest are met more than half way.

The early romances, the prototypes of the modern novel, from "Don Quixote" to "Tom Jones" and "Joseph Andrews," were little more than narratives of adventures on the road. "Joseph Andrews" in particular--perhaps Fielding's masterpiece--is simply the story of a journey from London to a place in the country some hundred and fifty miles distant. In these books all the adventures are associated with inns and the various characters, thrown together by chance, there assembled. Dickens unquestionably derived inspiration from Smollett and Fielding; nor is there any doubt but that Harte made a close study of Dickens.

From which preamble we come to the statement; if you would study human nature on the road, you must simply go where men congregate and exchange ideas. The plots of nearly all Bret Harte's mining stories are thus closely associated with the bar-rooms and taverns of the mining towns of his day. What would remain of any of Phillpott's charming stories of rural England, if you eliminated the bar-room of the village inn? In hospitality and generous living, the inns of the mining towns still keep up the old traditions. The card room and bar-room are places where men meet; to altogether avoid them from any pharisaical assumption of moral superiority is to lose the chance of coming in contact with the leading citizen, philanthropist, or eccentric character.

In the old romances it must be admitted there is much brawling and heavy drinking, as well as unseemliness of conduct. Yet in spite of the fact that hotel bars and saloons abound in all the old mining towns, the writer throughout his travels and notwithstanding the intense heat, not only saw no person under the influence of liquor, but also never heard a voice raised in angry dispute. Moderation, decency and a kindly consideration for the rights of others seem habitual with these people.

It is fifteen miles from Grass Valley to Smartsville, and I arrived at the Smartsville Hotel in time for the midday meal. Smartsville has "seen better days," but still maintains a cheerful outlook on life. The population has dwindled from several thousand to about three hundred. It is, however, the central point for quite an extensive agricultural and pastoral country surrounding it.

The swinging sign over the hotel bears the legend, "Smartsville Hotel, John Peardon, Propr." The present proprietor is named "Peardon," but everyone addressed him as "Jim." Having established a friendly footing, I said: "Mr. Peardon, I notice the sign over the door reads John Peardon. How is it that they all call you 'Jim?'" "Oh," he replied, "John Peardon was my father, I was born in this hotel;"--another of the numerous instances that came under my observation of the way these people "stay where they are put."

John Peardon was an Englishman. The British Isles furnished a very considerable percentage of the pioneers, the evidences whereof remain unto this day. The swinging signs over the hotels for one; another, the prevalence in all the mining towns of Bass's pale ale. You will find it in the most unpretentious hotels and restaurants. An Englishman expects his ale or beer, as a matter of course, whether at the Equator or at the Arctic Circle. When I first arrived in California in 1868, I drifted down into the then sheep and cattle country in the lower end of Monterey County. An English family living on an isolated ranch sent home for a girl who had worked for them in the old country. Upon her arrival, the first question she asked was: "How far is it to the church?" The second: "Where can I get my beer?" When informed there was no church within a hundred miles and that it was at least fifteen miles to the nearest saloon, the poor woman felt that she was indeed all abroad! Bereft, at one blow of the Established Church and English Ale, the solid ground seemed to have given way from under her feet. For her, these two particulars comprised the whole of the British Constitution.

Smartsville possessed a sentimental interest for me, for the reason that in the sixties my father mined and taught a private school in an adjoining camp bearing the derogatory appellation "Sucker Flat." What mischance prompted this title will never now be known. In my father's time, it contained a population of nearly a thousand persons; and judging from the manner in which the gulch and the contiguous flat have been torn, scarred, burrowed into and tunneled under, if gold there was, most strenuous efforts had been made to bring it to light.

I asked if there was anyone in Smartsville who would be likely to remember my father, and was referred by Mr. Peardon to "Bob" Beatty, who, he said, had, lived in Smartsville all his life and knew everybody. As Mr. Beatty was within a stone's throw, at the Excelsior Store, I had no difficulty in finding him. Introducing myself, I asked Mr. Beatty if he remembered my father. "To be sure I do," he exclaimed, "I went to his school, and," laughing heartily, "well I remember a licking he gave me!" He said that among the boys who attended that school, several in after years, as men, had become prominent in the history of the State.

Mr. Beatty--now a pleasant, genial gentleman of fifty-two--very kindly walked with me to the brow of the hill commanding a view of Sucker Flat, and pointed out the exact spot where the school had stood, for not a stick or a stone remains to mark the locus of the town--it is simply a name upon the map.

I mention this incident as being another proof of the extraordinary hold the Sierra foot-hill country has upon the people who were born there, as well as upon those who have drifted there by force of circumstances. It is forty-six or forty-seven years since my father conducted that school, yet I felt so sure from previous experiences there would be in Smartsville someone who remembered him, that I determined to include it in my itinerary.

Chapter VIII
Smartsville to Marysville. Some Reflections on Automobiles and "Hoboes"

Early the next morning I started for Marysville, the last leg in my journey, and a long twenty miles distant. I had been dreading the pull through the Sacramento Valley, having a lively recollection of my experience in the San Joaquin, on leaving Stockton. The day was sultry, making the heat still more oppressive. After leaving the foot-hills for good, I walked ten miles before reaching a tree, or anything that cast a shadow, if you except the telephone poles. For the first time I realized there was danger in walking in such heat, and even contemplated the shade of the telephone poles as a possibility! Fortunately a light breeze sprang up--the fag end of the trade wind--and, though hot, it served to dispel that stagnation of the atmosphere which in sultry weather is so trying to the nervous system. Marysville is nearly one hundred miles due north of Stockton--of course, much farther by rail--and the same arid, treeless, inhospitable belt of country between the cultivated area and the foot-hills apparently extends the whole distance. It is a country to avoid.

About two miles short of Marysville, while enjoying the shade cast by the trees that border the levee of the Feather River, which skirts Marysville to the south, a man in an auto stopped and very kindly offered to give me a lift. I thanked him politely but declined. He seemed amazed. "Why don't you ride when you can?" he asked. "Because I prefer to walk," I answered. This fairly staggered him. The idea of a man preferring to walk, and in such heat, was probably a novel experience, and served to deprive him of further speech. He simply sat and stared and I had passed him some twenty yards before he started his machine.

A sturdy tramp walking in the middle of the road, who had witnessed the scene, shouted as he passed: "Why didn't yer ride wid de guy?" I replied as before, "Because I prefer to walk;" adding for his benefit, "I've no use for autos." Whereupon he threw back his head and burst into peal after peal of such hearty laughter that, from pure contagion, I perforce joined in the chorus. In the days of Fielding and Sam Johnson, this fellow would have been dubbed "a lusty vagabond;" in the slangy parlance of today, he was a "husky hobo," equipped as such, even to the tin can of the comic journals. To him, the humor of a brother tramp refusing a ride--in an autocar, at that--appealed with irresistible force.

To walk in the middle of the road is characteristic of the genuine tramp. There must be some occult reason for this peculiarity, since in a general way, it is far easier going on the margin. Perhaps it is because he commands a better view of either side, with a regard to the possible onslaught of dogs. There is something about a man with a pack on his back that infuriates the average dog, as I have on several occasions found to my annoyance. Robert Louis Stevenson, in his whimsical and altogether delightful "Travels with a Donkey," thus vents his opinion anent the dog question:

"I was much disturbed by the barking of a dog, an animal that I fear more than any wolf. A dog is vastly braver and is, besides, supported by a sense of duty. If you kill a wolf you meet with encouragement and praise, but if you kill a dog, the sacred rights of property and the domestic affections come clamoring around you for redress. At the end of a fagging day, the sharp, cruel note of a dog's bark is in itself a keen annoyance; and to a tramp like myself, he represents the sedentary and respectable world in its most hostile form. There is something of the clergyman or the lawyer about this engaging animal; and if he were not amenable to stones, the boldest man would shrink from traveling a-foot. I respect dogs much in the domestic circle; but on the highway or sleeping afield, I both detest and fear them."

I confess to a feeling of sympathy with the men we so indiscriminately brand with the contemptuous epithet, "hobo." In the first place, the road itself, with its accompanying humors and adventures, forms a mutual and efficacious bond. How little we know of the "Knights of the Road," or the compelling circumstances that turned them adrift upon the world! "All sorts and conditions of men" are represented, from the college professor to the ex-pugilist. I have "hit the ties" in company with a so-called "hobo" who quoted Milton and Shakespeare by the yard, interspersed with exclamations appreciative of his enjoyment of the country through which we were passing. And once when on a tramp along the coast from San Francisco to Monterey, I fell in at Point San Pedro with a professional, who bitterly regretted the coming of the Ocean Shore Railway, then in process of construction.

"For years," said he, "I have been in the habit of making this trip at regular intervals, on my way south. I had the road to myself and thoroughly enjoyed the peaceful beauty of the scene; but now this railroad has come with its mushroom towns, and all the charm has gone. Never again for me! This is my last trip!"

I have not the slightest doubt that sheer love of the road--and only a tramp knows what those words mean--is the controlling influence which keeps fifty per cent of the fraternity its willing slaves. What was Senhouse--that most fascinating of Maurice Hewlett's creations--but a tramp? A gentleman tramp, if you please, but still a tramp. What is the reason that Senhouse appeals so strongly to the imagination? Simply because he loved Nature. And in this matter-of-fact period when poetry is dead and even a by-word, the man who loves Nature, if not a poet, at least has poetry in his soul. In a decadent age symbolized by the tango and the problem play, it is at least an encouraging sign for the future that such a character as Senhouse came to the jaded reader of the erotic fiction of the day, as a whiff of sea breeze on a parched plain, and was hailed with corresponding delight.

Of course there are "hoboes" and "hoboes," as in any other profession, but so far as my experience goes, the "hobo" is an idealist. Of the many reasons he has taken to the road, not the least is the freedom from the shackles of convention and the "Gradgrind" methods of an utilitarian and materialistic age. Nor is he a pessimist. Whatever his trouble, the road has eased him of his burden and made him a philosopher.

Thoreau, writing in the middle of the last century, deplores the fact that in his day, as now, but few of his countrymen took any pleasure in walking, and that very rarely one encountered a person with any real appreciation of the beauty of Nature, which if he could but see it, lay at his very door. Speaking for himself and companion in his rambles, he says: "We have felt that we almost alone hereabouts (Concord, Massachusetts) practiced this noble art; though, to tell the truth, at least if their own assertions are to be received, most of my townsmen would fain walk sometimes, as I do, but they cannot. No wealth can buy the requisite leisure, freedom and independence which are the capital in this profession. It comes only by the grace of God. It requires a direct dispensation from Heaven to become a Walker. Ambulator nascitur non fit. Some of my townsmen, it is true, can remember and have described to me, walks which they took ten years ago, in which they were so blessed as to lose themselves for half an hour in the woods."

Who is there who walks habitually, who does not know the man who tells you of the walks he "used to take?" You have known him, say a dozen years. During all that time, to your knowledge, his walks have practically been limited by the distance to his office and back from the ferry boat. When you urge him for perhaps the twentieth time, to essay a tramp with you, he will say he would like to very much, but unfortunately so-and-so renders it impossible. And then looking you in the eye, he will tell you how much he enjoyed tramps he took, of twenty or thirty miles--but that was before you knew him! As if a Walker with a big "W," as Thoreau writes the word, would remain satisfied with the memory of walks of twenty years ago!

I had heard of the "Marysville Buttes," as one has heard of Madagascar, but their actual appearance on the landscape came as the greatest surprise of the trip. As I first caught sight of them when within a few miles of Marysville, they gave me a distinct thrill. I could hardly believe my eyes and thought of mirages; for those pointed, isolated peaks rise precipitously from the floor of the Sacramento valley; in fact, their bases are only a mile or two from the river. They have every indication, even to the unscientific eye, of having been upheaved by volcanic action. Perhaps that accounts for the uncanny impression they impart.

A walk of twenty-one or two miles without food, in any kind of weather, is apt to produce an aching void. My first efforts on reaching Marysville were therefore directed to finding the sort of place where I could eat in comfort. The emphasis which Robert Louis Stevenson employs when upon this most important quest would be amusing were it not also a vital problem in your own case. There is nothing humorous per se in hunger or thirst; at any rate, not until both are appeased. With the black coffee and cigar, you can tip your chair at a comfortable angle against the wall, and watching the delicate wreaths of smoke in their spiral upward course, previous to final disintegration, smile at the persistent energy with which an hour ago you systematically worked the town from end to end, anxiously peering in the windows of uninviting restaurants until you finally found that little "hole in the wall" for which you were looking, with the bottle of Tipo Chianti, the succulent chops and the big red tomatoes, in the window. It is always to be found if you have the necessary perseverance. The genial Italian proprietor, with the innate politeness of his countrymen, will not bore you with questions as to where you have come from, whither you are going, or what you are walking for, anyway, etc., etc. He accepts you just as you are--haversack, camera, big stick and all, hanging them without comment on the hook behind your head; while you simply tell him you want a good dinner, the best he can give you, but to include the chops, tomatoes and Tipo Chianti. With a smile and that artistic flip of the napkin under his arm, which only he can achieve, he sets about giving his orders. Later on, after a hot bath, a shave and the luxury of a clean shirt, feeling at peace with the world and refreshed in body and soul, you set out to examine the town in comfort and at your leisure.

In the mining days, Marysville ranked next to San Francisco, Sacramento and possibly Stockton, not only in interest but in actual volume of business transacted. It was the natural outlet for all the foot-hill country tributary to Grass Valley, Nevada City, and Smartsville. There the miners outfitted and there, when they had "made their pile," they began the process--subsequently completed in Sacramento and San Francisco--of reducing it to a negligible quantity. That, of course, is merely a reminiscence, but as the center of one of the most prosperous grain and fruit-raising sections of the Sacramento Valley, Marysville is still a place of considerable importance. The old town is very much in evidence; so much so that, in spite of the numerous modern buildings, the general effect produced is of age, as age is understood in California. I doubt if San Francisco before the fire, or Sacramento today, could show as many substantial, solid buildings dating back to the fifties.

Chapter IX
Bayard Taylor and the California of Forty-Nine. Bret Harte and His Literary Pioneer Contemporaries.

And here in old Marysville, the county seat of Yuba County and situated on its extreme western boundary, I ended my tramp, having covered a distance of approximately two hundred and fifty miles, exclusive of retracements. The ideal time to visit the Sierra foot-hills would be in the late Spring or early Autumn. I was compelled to grasp the opportunity when it offered or forego the pleasure altogether. Nor is it necessary, of course, to walk; the roads, whilst generally speaking not classed as good going for automobiles, are at least passable. I was surprised at the number of high grade machines in evidence, in all the towns of importance mentioned in this narrative. There remains also the alternative of a good saddle horse, or, better still, a light wagon with camping outfit, thus rendering hotels unnecessary, the elimination of which would probably pay the hire of horse and wagon.

Half a century is a long period. You could probably count on the fingers of one hand persons now living in the Sierra foot-hills who have any recollection of ever having seen Bret Harte. It must also be remembered that in the fifties his reputation as an author had not been established. Of all that group of brilliant young men who visited the mines in early days, which included for a brief space "Orpheus C. Kerr" and "Artemus Ward," I can well imagine that Bret Harte attracted the least attention. It is extremely doubtful to my mind if he ever had much actual experience of the mining camps. To a man of his vivid imagination, a mere suggestion afforded a plot for a story; even the Laird's Toreadors, it will be recalled, were commercially successful when purely imaginary; he only failed when he subsequently studied the real thing in Spain.

Bret Harte was a man who in a primitive community might well escape notice. In appearance, manner and training, he was the exact antithesis of Mark Twain. He was a student before he was a writer and possessed the student's shy reserve. I can well imagine him, a slight boyish figure, flitting from camp to camp, wrapped in his own thoughts, keeping his own counsel. Yet he alone of that little band, unless you except Mark Twain, possessed the divine spark we call "genius." Centuries after the names of all the rest are buried in oblivion, Bret Harte's stories of the Argonauts in the mining towns of California will remain the classics they have already become.

Yet as before stated, when once I got fairly started on the road, the pioneers themselves and their worthy descendants absorbed my interest and assumed the center of the stage to the exclusion, for the time being, of the romancers; who, after all, each in his own fashion, depicted only what most appealed to him in the characters of these same men and their contemporaries. Bayard Taylor in his interesting work "El Dorado," the first edition of which appeared in 1850, thus states his opinion of the men of '49:

"Abundance of gold does not always beget, as moralists tell us, a grasping and avaricious spirit. The principles of hospitality were as faithfully observed in the rude tents of the diggers, as they could be by the thrifty farmers of the North and West. The cosmopolitan cast of character in California, resulting in the commingling of so many races, and the primitive mode of life, gave a character of good-fellowship to all its members; and in no part of the world have I ever seen help more freely given to the needy, or more ready co-operation in any human proposition. Personally, I can safely say that I never met with such unvarying kindness from comparative strangers."

That last sentence also spelt the literal truth in my experience. Even the dogs were kindly disposed and though I carried, a "big stick," except by way of companionship and as an aid in climbing, I might safely have left it at home. And while at times I walked through a wild, mountainous and almost deserted country, the idea of possible danger never occurred to me. When finally one encountered a human being, he invariably proved a courteous, obliging and companionable personage to meet.

Bayard Taylor attended in September and the beginning of October, 1849, the convention at Monterey, which gave to California its first, and in the opinion of many, its best constitution. He closes his review of the proceedings with these forceful and prophetic words:

"Thus we have another splendid example of the ease and security with which people can be educated to govern themselves. From that chaos whence under, a despotism like the Austrian, would spring the most frightful excesses of anarchy and crime, a population of freemen peacefully and quietly develops the highest form of civil order--the broadest extent of liberty and security. Governments, bad and corrupt as many of them are, and imperfect as they all must necessarily be, nevertheless at times exhibit scenes of true moral sublimity. What I have today witnessed has so, impressed me; and were I a believer in omens, I would augur from the tranquil beauty of the evening--from the clear sky and the lovely sunset hues on the waters of the bay--more than all, from the joyous expression of every face I see, a glorious and prosperous career for the State of California."

Southern California, by which is understood all of the State south of the Tehachapi Mountains, was mostly settled by and is still to a great extent the objective point of people from the East and Middle West. Most of them came in search of health and brought a competency sufficient for their needs. When President Wilson, then Governor of New Jersey, visited California in 1911, he came over the southern route to Los Angeles. Addressing a Pasadena audience he said: "I am much disappointed when I see you. I expected to find a highly individualized people, characters developed by struggle and mutual effort; but I find you the same people we have at home," and more, to the same effect. Subsequently, Governor Wilson delivered an address at the Greek Theater, Berkeley, before the students of the University of California. At its close, Mr. Maslin mounted the stage, a copy of the paper containing the account of the Pasadena speech in his hands, and asked the Governor if he was correctly reported; to which he replied in the affirmative. "Governor," said Mr. Maslin, "you came into the State at the wrong gate!" "Gate? gate?--what gate?" inquired the Governor. "You should have come through Emigrant Gap, through which most of the emigrants from '49 and on entered the State. Now, Governor, the people you saw at Pasadena never suffered the trials of a pioneer's lite, they are not knit together by the memory of mutual struggles and privations. When you come to the State again, come through Emigrant Gap. Let me know when you come, and I will introduce you to a breed of men the world has never excelled." With the smile with which millions have since become familiar, Governor Wilson grasped the hand of the pioneer and said: "When I come again, as I feel sure I shall, I shall let you know."

The following morning I took the train for my home in Alameda. As I sat and meditated on the scenes I had witnessed and the character of the people I had met, it was borne in upon me that this had been the most interesting as well as enjoyable experience of my life. Already the temporary discomforts produced by heat and soiled garments had faded into insignificance, and assumed a most trivial aspect when I reviewed the journey as a whole. They were part of the game. To again quote "Trilby," tramping "is not all beer and skittles." Your true tramp learns to take things as he finds them and never to expect or ask or the impossible. He will drink the wine of the country, even when sour, without a grimace; pass without grumbling a sleepless night; plod through dust ankle deep, without a murmur; there is but one vulnerable feature in his armor, and with Achilles, it is his heel! And it is literally the heel that, is the sensitive spot. I will venture the assertion that the long-distance tramper--not even excepting Brother Weston--who has not at some time or another suffered from sore heels, does not exist. The tramp's feet are his means of locomotion; on their condition he bestows an anxiety and care which far surpass that of the man in the automobile, with all his complicated machinery to inspect.

Remains then, the memory of the delicious, faint, cool, morning breeze, gently stirring the pine needles; the aromatic odor of forest undergrowth; the murmur of the stream hurrying down the mountain gorge to mingle its pure waters with those of the muddy Sacramento, far away in the great valley below; the deep awe-inspiring canons of the American, Stanislaus and Mokelumne Rivers; and back of all, the azure summits of the Sierra Nevada.

Remains also, the memory of the kindly-disposed, courteous and open-hearted inhabitants of the old mining towns. But more forcibly than all else combined--for it seems to epitomize the whole--the glamour of the towns themselves appeals with an irresistible fascination, that no poor words of mine can adequately express.

The Codes Of Hammurabi And Moses
W. W. Davies

QTY

The discovery of the Hammurabi Code is one of the greatest achievements of archaeology, and is of paramount interest, not only to the student of the Bible, but also to all those interested in ancient history...

Religion ISBN: *1-59462-338-4* Pages:132

MSRP ***$12.95***

The Theory of Moral Sentiments
Adam Smith

QTY

This work from 1749. contains original theories of conscience amd moral judgment and it is the foundation for systemof morals.

Philosophy ISBN: *1-59462-777-0* Pages:536

MSRP ***$19.95***

Jessica's First Prayer
Hesba Stretton

QTY

In a screened and secluded corner of one of the many railway-bridges which span the streets of London there could be seen a few years ago, from five o'clock every morning until half past eight, a tidily set-out coffee-stall, consisting of a trestle and board, upon which stood two large tin cans, with a small fire of charcoal burning under each so as to keep the coffee boiling during the early hours of the morning when the work-people were thronging into the city on their way to their daily toil...

Pages:84

Childrens ISBN: *1-59462-373-2*

MSRP ***$9.95***

My Life and Work
Henry Ford

QTY

Henry Ford revolutionized the world with his implementation of mass production for the Model T automobile. Gain valuable business insight into his life and work with his own auto-biography... "We have only started on our development of our country we have not as yet, with all our talk of wonderful progress, done more than scratch the surface. The progress has been wonderful enough but..."

Pages:300

Biographies/ ISBN: *1-59462-198-5*

MSRP ***$21.95***

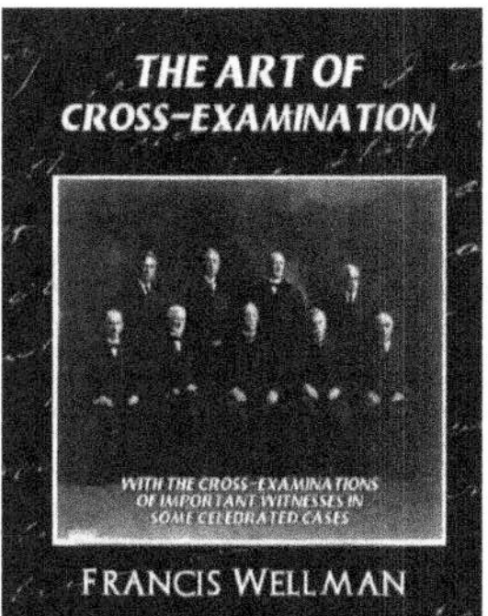

The Art of Cross-Examination
Francis Wellman

QTY

I presume it is the experience of every author, after his first book is published upon an important subject, to be almost overwhelmed with a wealth of ideas and illustrations which could readily have been included in his book, and which to his own mind, at least, seem to make a second edition inevitable. Such certainly was the case with me; and when the first edition had reached its sixth impression in five months, I rejoiced to learn that it seemed to my publishers that the book had met with a sufficiently favorable reception to justify a second and considerably enlarged edition. ..

Pages:412

Reference **ISBN:** ***1-59462-647-2*** *MSRP* ***$19.95***

On the Duty of Civil Disobedience

Henry David Thoreau

On the Duty of Civil Disobedience
Henry David Thoreau

QTY

Thoreau wrote his famous essay, On the Duty of Civil Disobedience, as a protest against an unjust but popular war and the immoral but popular institution of slave-owning. He did more than write—he declined to pay his taxes, and was hauled off to gaol in consequence. Who can say how much this refusal of his hastened the end of the war and of slavery ?

Law **ISBN:** ***1-59462-747-9*** Pages:48

MSRP ***$7.45***

Dream Psychology

Psychoanalysis for Beginners

Sigmund Freud

Dream Psychology Psychoanalysis for Beginners
Sigmund Freud

QTY

Sigmund Freud, born Sigismund Schlomo Freud (May 6, 1856 - September 23, 1939), was a Jewish-Austrian neurologist and psychiatrist who co-founded the psychoanalytic school of psychology. Freud is best known for his theories of the unconscious mind, especially involving the mechanism of repression; his redefinition of sexual desire as mobile and directed towards a wide variety of objects; and his therapeutic techniques, especially his understanding of transference in the therapeutic relationship and the presumed value of dreams as sources of insight into unconscious desires.

Pages:196

Psychology **ISBN:** ***1-59462-905-6*** *MSRP* ***$15.45***

The Miracle of Right Thought
Orison Swett Marden

QTY

Believe with all of your heart that you will do what you were made to do. When the mind has once formed the habit of holding cheerful, happy, prosperous pictures, it will not be easy to form the opposite habit. It does not matter how improbable or how far away this realization may see, or how dark the prospects may be, if we visualize them as best we can, as vividly as possible, hold tenaciously to them and vigorously struggle to attain them, they will gradually become actualized, realized in the life. But a desire, a longing without endeavor, a yearning abandoned or held indifferently will vanish without realization.

Pages:360

Self Help **ISBN:** ***1-59462-644-8*** *MSRP* ***$25.45***

www.ingramcontent.com/pod-product-compliance
Lightning Source LLC
Chambersburg PA
CBHW081201170626
46813CB00009B/3279
* 9 7 8 1 4 3 8 5 7 3 1 0 6 *